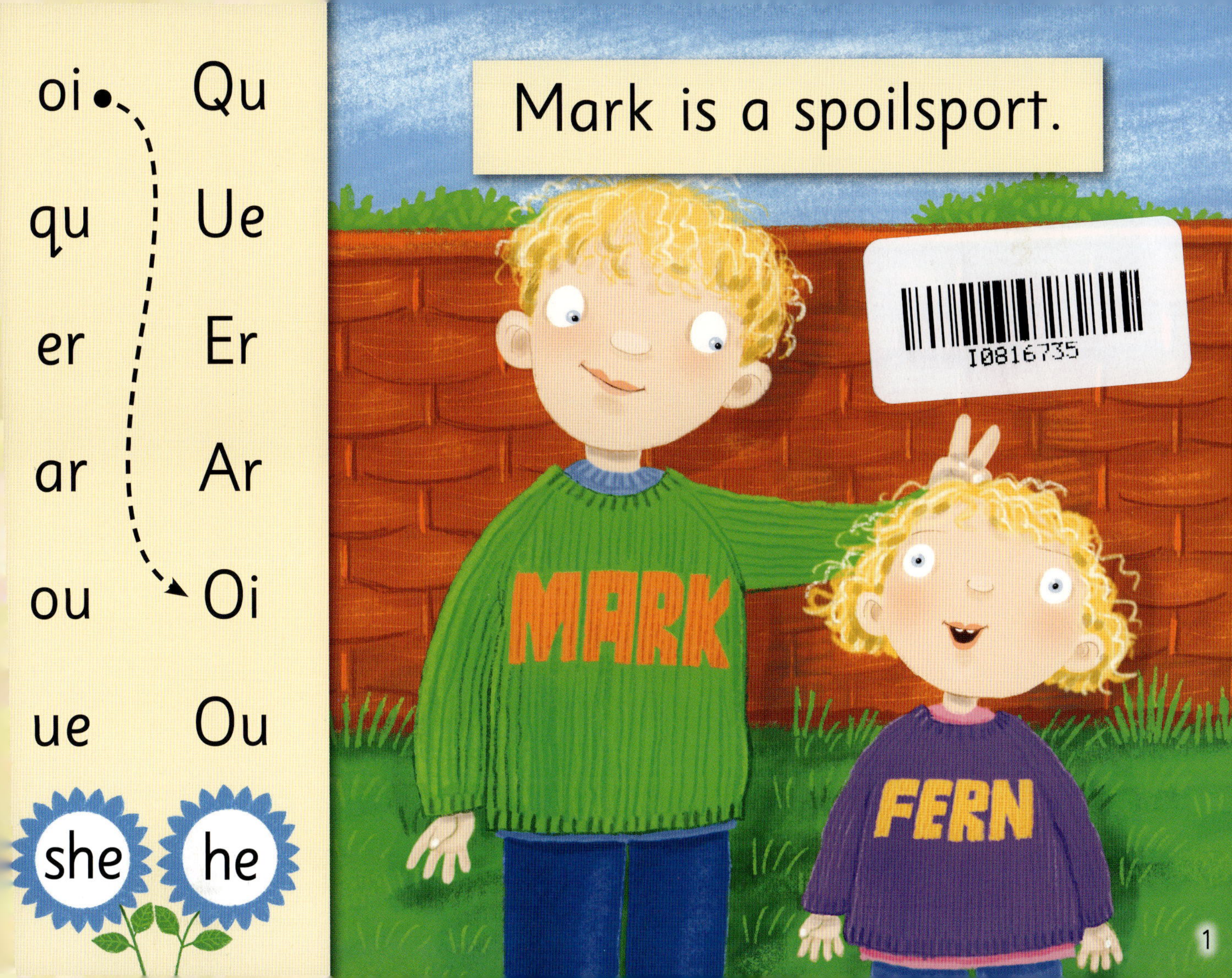
oi
qu
er
ar
ou
ue
Qu
Ue
Er
Ar
Oi
Ou
she
he
Mark is a spoilsport.
I0816735
MARK
FERN

He spoils his sister's fun.

"I can count better than Fern can!" he shouts.

And I am better at painting!

She will not win this quiz.
She is not clever.

This scooter is quicker than Fern's.

Mark whizzes along.

He speeds around the corner...

...and lands in the duck pond!

Dad rescues Mark from the pond.

Mark shivers on a park bench.

Fern is not quick, but she is much better at avoiding the pond!